What's Your Ford?

by Miss Bernacchia's class
with Tony Stead

capstone

Introduction

When Henry Ford invented his first gasoline-powered vehicle in 1896, he probably did not envision the modern vehicles we have today. His work with gasoline-powered engines set the stage for a whole new industry that would change the way that we travel for work and for fun. Learning about his invention got us thinking. What other inventions impact our lives? We decided to do some research about important inventions and write about some of our favorites. What's YOUR Ford?

Our Favorite Inventions

Year	Invention
1783	Hot-air Balloons
1927	TVs
1930	Trampolines
1946	Credit and Debit Cards
1958	Video Games
1968	Video Game Consoles
1971	E-mail
2000	Tablets

Hot-air Balloon

by Royal

Have you ever given any thought to the invention of the first hot-air balloon? How did it lift an enormous balloon plus the weight of people into the sky? To learn more about this fascinating ball of gas, keep reading. You'll find out who made the first hot-air balloon, the challenges, and the reasons people dare to take a ride! This really is one of my favorite inventions.

The first hot-air balloon was invented by French brothers Joseph and Etienne Montgolfier. Jean-Franíçois Pilatre De Rozier and Marquis d'Arlandes were the first to test it. The date was September 19, 1783. The first passengers were a sheep, a duck, and a rooster! The flight lasted about 10 minutes before the balloon crashed to the ground. But the animals survived. During another flight two years later, De Rozier was killed trying to cross the English Channel. His balloon exploded only 30 minutes into his flight. As time passed new records were set for the highest hot-air balloon flight as well as the time spent in the air. In 1987 Richard Branson and Per Lindstrand were the first to fly across the Atlantic Ocean in a hot-air balloon.

illustrated by Cassandra

The hot-air balloon has many challenges. First, wind conditions can affect the balloon. Too much wind, or gusts of wind, can make the balloon travel too far or cause it to have problems landing. Wind can also cave in the side of the balloon when it is being filled by heated air. This can cause the balloon to roll around on the ground and put people in danger. The temperature outside also changes the flight of the balloon. If the weather is too hot or too cold, the balloon can fly at different heights and speeds. Being able to predict the weather helps pilots decide when to fly.

Today, hot-air balloons are used mostly for entertainment and sightseeing. People go on hot-air balloon rides for parties, dates, honeymoons, and the best of all—weddings! There are hot-air balloon festivals all over the world. For example, the Michigan Challenge Balloonfest is held in Howell, Michigan, and includes more than 50 balloons. It is a way to get the community together.

For more than 220 years, the world has been able to enjoy the scenery from hundreds of feet above the ground thanks to hot-air balloons. Next time you look into the sky and see a massive balloon floating by, you can appreciate how long the hot-air balloon has been around and how patient new inventors need to be to make their inventions a success!

envelope (balloon
holds in hot air)
burner (heats
the air)
gondola (basket
carries passengers)

The First TV

by Edrik

For almost 90 years, people have been able to sit down and relax in front of the TV. Have you ever stopped to think about who invented the very first TV? Keep reading to find out about my favorite invention. Learn who invented the TV, why it's important to our society, and how it is used for education.

In 1927 Philo Farnsworth invented the first electronic television in San Francisco, California. One story is that Philo actually got his inspiration while working in a field of vegetables! He figured out that a picture could be broken down into lines of electricity similar to the plow rows in the field. If the lines were shown really fast, they could come together as a whole picture when viewed by the human eye. That was the beginning, but Philo alone did not invent the television as we know it. It took many scientists, inventors, and artists for the TV to evolve.

The original intent of the television was not for entertainment but to share information through pictures and sound together. But it sure has evolved to become entertainment! Families around the world enjoy sitcoms, sporting events, movies, and concerts on a daily basis.

TV is a quick way to get information out to lots of people. It keeps us up to date about the current happenings around the globe. News programs are on multiple times during the day and night, reporting on local, national, and worldly events. Documentaries, travel, cooking, and other educational programs can help people of all ages to educate themselves in many different areas of life. According to the Federal Communications Commission, children in the United States spend more than three hours a day on average watching TV. We can only hope that they are watching the educational shows rather than shows that lead to violence and bad behavior.

We can thank the efforts of Philo Farnsworth for his work on the first television, but let's not forget that it was the teamwork of many that helped this much-appreciated invention evolve! TV is more important today than ever before. We rely on that little (or big) box to send us knowledge, information, and up-to-date news. I'm not quite sure what I would do without it. How about you?

Trampoline

By Laisha

Fact: Jumping on a trampoline for 30 minutes can burn more than 100 calories! Can you believe something so fun is a great form of exercise? *Reader's Digest* has reported that NASA found bouncing on a trampoline to be better exercise than jogging by 68 percent. Kids and adults all over the world enjoy bouncing on trampolines. Keep reading to find out who created the first trampoline, how safe they are, and the health benefits of all that bouncing! No wonder I like trampolines so much!

In the 1930s, George Nissen built the first modern trampoline in his garage in Iowa. He built it by pulling a canvas sheet over a rectangular steel frame. As the idea evolved, Nissen and gymnastic coach Larry Griswold used inner tubes from tires to attach the canvas to the frame to give it more bounce. That idea ultimately resulted in the use of springs so people could jump much higher. At first trampolines were used to train astronauts and as tools for different kinds of sports. Trampolining gained popularity when Nissen bounced on a trampoline alongside a kangaroo! Who wouldn't want to feel what it's like to be a kangaroo?

Even though trampolining is fun, it wasn't the safest invention. The frame and springs are made out of metal, and there are holes near the springs where people can fall through or get stuck. The bottom of the trampoline is very unstable, so it is possible for a trampoline to collapse. However, another kind of trampoline was developed called the springless trampoline. This is a safer trampoline. There are no metal springs, and there are no holes inside the net to fall through.

Jumping on a trampoline is a way to exercise. Trampolining builds coordination, strength, and balance. Some people have mini trampolines inside their homes that they use for exercise. You can regularly find adults taking trampoline workout classes at their local gyms. Gymnastic coaches use the trampoline during practice sessions to help strengthen the leg muscles of the training gymnasts. Not only is trampolining fun, it is a great way to motivate yourself to be healthy. You can still chat with a friend, listen to music, or watch television while bouncing and making yourself healthier!

George Nissen was an amazing inventor who helped to give our world a bit more fun. Who would have thought that a human could have the experience of bouncing like a kangaroo? The trampoline gave the world a new way to exercise, train, and have a great time while doing it.

illustrated by Geniya

Credit and Debit Cards

By Isabelle C.

Did you know that in 2014 there were more than 800 million Visa credit cards worldwide? If you want to learn about how the credit card came into existence, pros and cons of using a credit card, how the credit card makes our lives simpler, and why people use debit cards instead of credit cards, then keep reading!

The idea of using credit toward purchases goes back hundreds of years. It wasn't uncommon for a farmer to get things on credit at local stores. The farmer would pay later for what was owed. Then John Biggins created the credit card in 1946. He called this new concept Charg-It, and it was only offered to local customers who had money at his bank. In 1959 American Express made one of the first plastic cards.

Today, there are many pros and cons to using a credit card. Some of the good reasons to use a credit card are that it is convenient and easy to keep track of usage, and it can be used immediately. If you have an emergency and need to fly out to see a family member, you don't have to worry about having the money right then to afford the plane ticket. You can worry about the payment later! The credit card company sends out a statement each month, letting you know what you owe, which helps you organize and budget your money.

Of course, there is a downside to the credit card, too. Some people have too many credit cards. That can be a problem because when you get your credit card bills, you might not have the money to pay them all. And if you don't pay the minimum payment on time, there are late payment fees. If you don't pay the whole bill, you also have to pay interest to the credit card company. And some of those fees are really high.

Some people choose to use a debit card instead of a credit card. When you use a debit card, you take out as much money as you need from your bank account to pay for what you buy. That puts a limit on your spending because you can't buy more than you can afford. Another way you can use debit cards is to get money at Automated Teller Machines (ATMs), which are available all over the world. These machines are helpful because when you put the card inside the machine, you can take out money from your bank account in cash!

It's all about convenience and safety. Credit cards and debit cards have become a way of life. Some people feel safer with plastic than they do carrying around cash. If your wallet is full of cash and is lost or stolen, it is not replaceable whereas a wallet full of credit cards and debit cards can be cancelled in a heartbeat.

Can you believe how much we rely on plastic today? This way of charging has helped us get things that we want or need right away, but it can also get us into financial trouble if we're not careful! When you buy only what you can pay for, this invention makes it easier and sometimes safer to pay.

The First Video Game and Console

By Isabel T.

Long before there were video games, children used to play Ping-pong and board games. Children also played sports outside. Kids still do these things today, but they have other options, too. Let's step back in time to when the video game console was invented, and see what the fun is all about.

The person who invented the first video game was a physicist named William Higinbotham in the year 1958. It was invented at Brookhaven National Laboratory, which is located in Upton, New York. In 1968 Ralph Baer invented the first video game console. He also invented a video game that could connect to the television. This video game console was called the Brown Box. Games that were played on the Brown Box included Ping-pong using dots and lines on the screen.

Let's zoom into 1989 when the portable device called Game Boy hit the market. This was the first handheld portable device. There was one problem though: You could only see images in black and white, not color! In 1998 color came out and the crowd went wild! A total of more than 118 million Game Boys and Game Boy Colors were sold. Everyone thought that this was the ultimate creation—until inventors wowed us again.

In 2001 the first Xbox came out. This console's system had better performance than other consoles like it. At the release, there were several games to choose from, and it had the ability to play a DVD. It also became known for Xbox Live, which meant players could play online with real people from all over the world.

As more game consoles are created, advanced technology provides better and better graphics and more capabilities. We can now play games on our smartphones and tablets. If you are as into game consoles as I am, I bet you can't wait to see what they think of next!

E-mail

By Laisha

Have you ever wondered how we used to communicate before we had modern technology? Remember how we used to have to wait for the mail carrier to deliver our mail? Now we are lucky to talk with our friends through electronic mail! Keep on reading to find out why e-mail is an important invention. You'll learn some background about e-mail, including how it developed and why it is important.

The creator of e-mail is Ray Tomlinson. He sent the first e-mail in 1971. Tomlinson was a graduate of MIT and worked for a company called Raytheon. He invented software so that messages could be sent to users on other computers. Even though he invented e-mail, he was most known for making the @ sign in e-mail addresses.

Ray Tomlinson didn't want to use a word that could be a part of a person's username. And he wanted to use the word "at," so it identified where you can find the person. That's how the @ sign became a part of a person's e-mail address.

You Got Mail
@

Today, over 200 billion e-mails are sent and received a day. E-mail is used for many different purposes. We can contact friends, communicate with teachers, request information, and apply for jobs. Some e-mails are meant for advertising different products, stores, or activities. E-mail is a great way to get a message across when you need to send a document electronically or reach a lot of people with the same information. But remember your audience when writing. Using emoticons and abbreviations are fine for your friends but not necessarily for your principal!

Can you believe how much our communication system has changed in only a short few years? E-mail has helped us communicate with our friends and family about something important or serious. With all the technology advancements, think what the future can hold!

The Invention of Tablets

by Dakota

Have you ever thought about the invention of tablets? Who had the brilliant idea to have our technological resources at our fingertips at all times? Keep reading to find out who created the first tablet, what a tablet is used for, and the benefits of buying a tablet.

The person who invented the tablet is often debated. Some report that it was Steve Jobs, and others say it was Bill Gates. The unofficial findings are that Bill Gates created the tablet about a decade before Jobs, but it wasn't marketed well and failed. Both men wanted to use a computer that did not have a mouse or keyboard so that the device was not so difficult to transport. Whichever person you believe had the original idea, he was a genius!

The first tablet was like pencil and paper only on a screen. It was designed for people to write on using their fingers instead of a pen or pencil. Today, tablets respond to touch and have built-in keyboards that pop up when you need to search for something on the Internet or respond to an e-mail. There are many things that you can access on a tablet that you use on a computer. Tablets are used to help young kids learn how to use a device before moving on to a computer or video game console.

TABLET

Why would people buy tablets if they already have smartphones or computers? The answer is simple. A tablet is easy to use at school or at work to take notes or send a short e-mail. It is nice to open up an entire website rather than just use an app. Plus, it is light enough to carry. I bet a math book is heavier! A tablet also has a large screen, so people can easily download and watch their favorite movies or play their favorite video games.

Because of Bill Gates and Steve Jobs, we now have a new device that is light, easy to use and more practical than an awkward laptop. As more changes are made, tablets may become better and even easier to use.

Conclusion

From the first TV to e-mail, inventions have changed our lives for the better. Some of them are small things and others are huge inventions that changed the course of history. Most inventions make our lives easier or give us more entertainment. All inventions have helped make the things we use in our lives better and better. Think about the inventions that are part of your everyday life. What would your life be without them? What invention do you think should be created next?